Miranda's Smile

Miranda's Smile

THOMAS LOCKER

DIAL BOOKS / NEW YORK

Published by Dial Books
A Division of Penguin Books USA Inc.
375 Hudson Street
New York, New York 10014

Copyright © 1994 by Thomas Locker
All rights reserved
Designed by Nancy R. Leo
Printed in Hong Kong
by South China Printing Company (1988) Limited
First Edition
1 3 5 7 9 10 8 6 4 2

Library of Congress Cataloging in Publication Data
Locker, Thomas, 1937-
Miranda's smile / by Thomas Locker.–1st ed.
p.   cm.
Summary: Miranda's father, who is painting her portrait,
tries to capture the essence of her wonderful smile.
ISBN 0-8037-1688-5 (trade).–ISBN 0-8037-1689-3 (library)
[1. Smile–Fiction.   2. Artists–Fiction.   3. Fathers and daughters–Fiction.]
I. Title.
PZ7.L7945Mi 1994   [E]–dc20   93-28050   CIP   AC

The art for each picture consists of an oil painting that
is color-separated and reproduced in full color.

To Debbie

ॐ

Miranda's father was an artist and he worked at home.
When he tasted one of the chocolate chip cookies that Miranda had
just baked, he said, "This is without a doubt the finest cookie in the
entire world." Miranda smiled because he always said that, even
when the cookies were a little burnt on the bottom.

"What a wonderful smile you have," her father said, looking at
her affectionately. "I'd love to paint a picture that captures that
special look."

Miranda had always hoped her father would paint a picture of her. She ran to her room and changed into her favorite skirt and blue blouse. When she returned, her father began to draw. He drew all afternoon. But as the light began to fade, Miranda discovered to her dismay that one of her front teeth was getting loose.

Miranda didn't say anything to her father about the tooth, and prayed that it wouldn't fall out before he finished her portrait. She tried to keep smiling as he painted, but that day and the next she sensed that he wasn't happy with the picture.

"What's the matter, Daddy?" she asked him.

"There's something wrong with the smile," he said. "I can't seem to get it right."

The next morning it happened! There, beside the pillow, was Miranda's front tooth. She started to cry. What will happen to the painting? Why did my tooth have to fall out before Daddy finished my picture? All that day at school Miranda worried, but when she got home, she had an idea.

Before going to the studio Miranda baked another batch of cookies. When her father tasted one, he said, "This is without a doubt the finest cookie in the entire world." Miranda smiled–and her father saw the empty space between her teeth!

"Oh, no!" he exclaimed. "Now I'll never be able to get it." But Miranda walked straight over to the model's chair.

"Daddy, I can smile with my lips closed. Watch me," she said. The artist looked at his daughter and saw how much the painting meant to her, so he picked up his brushes and started to repaint the smile with the lips closed.

At first he said that it improved the painting, but he kept asking Miranda to come back the next day for a few final touches. This went on, day after day, for two weeks. Using tiny brushes he worked and reworked the mouth, getting more frustrated with each try.

Finally one afternoon he threw down his brushes. "I can't do it," he said in disgust. "I've done everything I know how—I still can't get it right though." Miranda pleaded with him to keep on trying, but he just stared silently at the painting.

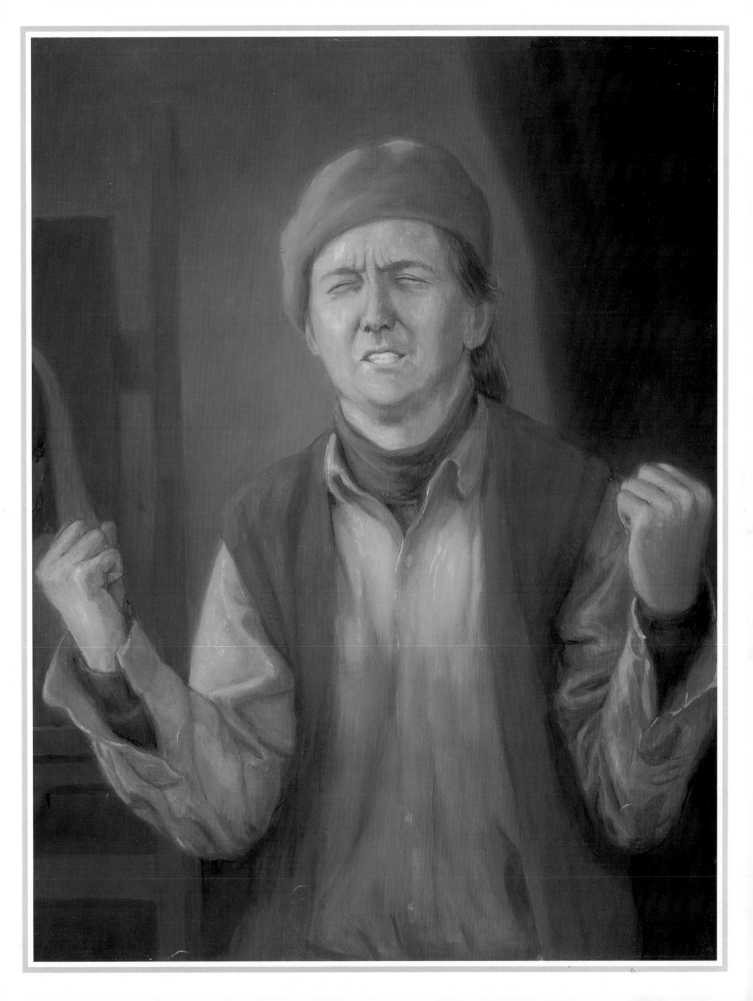

Miranda knew that her father wanted to be left alone. As she opened the studio door to leave, she decided that some cookies might cheer him up. Turning, she smiled at him. Her father looked up and nodded, then seemed startled.

As the door shut, he jumped up. "That's it! I know what it is! It's her eyes—the smile is in her eyes!" He returned to the portrait and his brushes flew. And the eyes in the painting began to smile.

Later Miranda returned with a plate of warm cookies just as her father stepped back to see if he had finally gotten the smile. And do you know what?

He had!

Miranda's father took her in his arms and tasted a cookie.

"This is without a doubt the best ever," he said. And do you know what? It was.

Thomas Locker first won awards for his illustrations in 1984, when Dial published his first book, *Where the River Begins*, which was named one of the year's Ten Best Illustrated books by *The New York Times*. It also received the *Parents' Choice* Award for Illustration and was praised in a starred *Booklist* review, which noted that the "spectacular paintings [are] reminiscent of nineteenth-century art." *The Land of Gray Wolf*, written as well as illustrated by Mr. Locker, was an *American Bookseller* Pick of the Lists. His most recently illustrated book for Dial is *The Ice Horse* by Candace Christiansen. His paintings are in many private collections and have been exhibited throughout the United States as well as in England. Mr. Locker lives in Stuyvesant, New York.